The Music Fairies

For Maddie Sparrow,
with lots of love

Special thanks to
Sue Mongredien

ORCHARD BOOKS
338 Euston Road, London NW1 3BH
Orchard Books Australia
Level 17/207 Kent Street, Sydney, NSW 2000
A Paperback Original

First published in 2008 by Orchard Books.

HiT entertainment

Illustrations © Orchard Books 2008

A CIP catalogue record for this book is available
from the British Library.

ISBN 978 1 40830 028 2
3 5 7 9 10 8 6 4 2

Printed and bound in China by Imago

Orchard Books is a division of Hachette Children's Books,
an Hachette UK company

www.hachette.co.uk

Danni
the Drum
Fairy

by Daisy Meadows

ORCHARD BOOKS

www.rainbowmagic.co.uk

I'm through with frost, ice and snow.
To the human world I must go!
I'll form a cool, Gobolicious Band.
Magical instruments will lend a hand.

With these instruments I'll go far.
Frosty Jack, a superstar.
I'll steal music's harmony and fun.
Watch out world, I'll be number one!

Contents

Extra-Exciting

"Bye, girls, I'll see you later," said Mrs Tate. "Have fun!"

"We will," Kirsty Tate replied, smiling. She leaned through the car window to kiss her mum goodbye. "Thanks for the lift. Bye!"

"Goodbye!" echoed Rachel Walker, Kirsty's best friend.

Both girls waved as Mrs Tate drove away. Kirsty looked up at the warehouse building they were standing in front of, and grinned at Rachel. "What are we waiting for?" she said. "Let's get inside!"

Rachel's eyes were bright as she slipped an arm through Kirsty's.

"I can't believe we're actually going to be in a pop video!" she said happily. "As if this holiday wasn't already brilliant enough!"

The two girls walked through tall glass double doors into the warehouse, feeling bubbly with anticipation. Rachel was staying with Kirsty's family for a week over the half-term holiday, and on the very first day the girls had found themselves in another of their wonderful fairy adventures. This time they had been helping the Music Fairies find their Magical Musical Instruments, which had been stolen by naughty Jack Frost and his goblins. So far, the girls had helped the Music Fairies find three of the instruments, but there were still four missing.

Today, Kirsty and Rachel were in for a very different kind of adventure, though. Kirsty felt dizzy with excitement as she thought about it again. She and Rachel were so lucky to be here. They were both big fans of Juanita, the pop star who'd shot to fame last year when she'd won the National Talent Competition. And now Juanita was making a video for her new song right here in Wetherbury! Not only that, but Mrs Tate's friend, Mandy, had been hired as the make-up artist for the video shoot...and she'd asked if Kirsty and Rachel would like to appear in the video as extras! Both girls were so excited and had been practising the routine at home as much as possible.

Kirsty's and Rachel's legs were trembling as they walked into the warehouse. They found themselves in a smart lobby area, with a reception desk plus a couple of bright red sofas. VIDEO SHOOT THIS WAY read a sign on the far wall, with an arrow pointing along a corridor.

"That's us," Rachel said, nudging Kirsty as she read the sign. There was a friendly-looking woman behind the reception desk, who smiled at the girls as they approached. "Hi," Kirsty said. "We're here as extras for the video."

"Great," the woman said, passing over a visitors' book. "If you could just sign in, I'll get someone to take you to the dressing rooms."

Kirsty and Rachel wrote down their names while the receptionist made a call. Then a woman in a purple mini-dress came along the corridor and smiled at them. "Hi, I'm Anna. Are you my extras?" she asked.

"Come with me, girls, and I'll show you your outfits."

Anna led Rachel and Kirsty to the wardrobe area, chatting as they walked. "We're having a bit of a nightmare today, but there's nothing for you two to worry about," she said. "It's just that the instruments don't seem to be working properly. We wanted to practise for the shoot with the musicians actually playing, but we've had to tell them to mime, instead."

Kirsty and Rachel exchanged glances. They knew why the instruments weren't working, of course – it was because some of the fairies' Magical Musical Instruments were still missing! The Music Fairies ensured that all music in Fairyland as well as the human world was fun to play, and sounded harmonious, but without their magical instruments, music didn't sound anywhere near as good.

Jack Frost knew this – and he also knew that while he and his goblins had the instruments, they'd be able to make fantastic music! The fairies had told Kirsty and Rachel that this was why he'd taken them in the first place – he'd formed a band and wanted to win next week's National Talent Competition. But if Jack Frost's group, Frosty and his Gobolicious Band, did win, it wouldn't take the press long to discover that Jack Frost wasn't human. And then, once the world knew that fairies existed, all of Kirsty's and Rachel's fairy friends would be in

terrible danger from
curious human beings!
  "Here we are!" said
Anna just then, opening
a door and leading
them into a room filled
with clothes rails.
There were all sorts of
colourful clothes and
accessories
hanging up, and racks
of shoes, too. Anna
pulled out a silver
glittery dress for
Kirsty and gave a
sequinned dress to
Rachel, then found
them both some shiny
pink platform boots.

Next she rummaged in a
large tea chest full of bright
scarves and hats, and
emerged with two
pairs of star-shaped
deely-boppers for
the girls to wear
on their heads.
"Funky, eh?"
Anna laughed.
"The song's
called *Cosmic
Craze*, that's
why we've got
everyone looking
a bit space-age."

The girls changed
their clothes quickly, then
Anna took them to Mandy's

make-up room. It was brightly
lit, with a huge mirror on
one wall, and two stools
set up in front of it.

"Hello there," Mandy
smiled. "Take a seat,
and I'll turn you into
little alien girls."

Kirsty and Rachel
both sat down and
Mandy set to work.
She dabbed some
glitter in their
eyebrows and painted
silvery swirls on their
cheeks. "Very cute," she
said. "Just a bit of sparkly
face powder, and you'll be
done."

She took out a silver pot of powder, and was about to lift the lid, when a stressed-looking man put his head around the door. "Mandy? Could you touch up Juanita's lipstick on set, please?"

"Sure," Mandy said at once. She passed the silver pot to Kirsty. "Would you mind dusting some of this over each other's faces, please, girls? I've got to go."

She bustled out of the room and Kirsty lifted the lid of the pot. As she did so, Danni the Drum Fairy burst out in a cloud of silver sparkles!

And... Action!

"Oooh!" Kirsty said in surprise. Then she smiled at the little fairy. "Hello again," she said. She and Rachel had met all of the Music Fairies at the start of the week.

Danni had long blonde hair swept off her face, and wore a short pink dress with a wide silver hem and neckline. She also had on a pair of black leggings and some pink pumps.

"Hi there," she said,
fluttering her wings to
shake off the sparkly
face powder. She gave
a dainty sneeze as the
powder floated all around
her. "I'm here to look for my Magic
Drums. I've got a feeling they're
somewhere nearby."

"Hi Danni," Rachel said. "We'll help
you look for your drums!"

"Girls, you're wanted on the set!"
came another voice just then, and
Mandy came back into the room.
Danni had to make a dive under
Kirsty's ponytail so as not to be seen.
Kirsty could feel the little fairy's wings
tickling the back of her neck as Mandy
took her and Rachel to where the video

was being filmed.

There was a stage area at the back of a large room, where a guitarist, keyboard player and drummer were positioned, with bright lights shining down on them. Glowing stars and planets dangled above their heads, and they were all wearing silver robot costumes. In the centre of the stage was Juanita, wearing a shimmering turquoise dress, her long black hair rippling down her back.

"Wow," Kirsty breathed, staring at the singer in awe. It was amazing to think that Kirsty and Rachel were going to be sharing a stage with such a famous person!

The stressed man they'd seen earlier told the two friends where to stand at the back of the set and when they should start performing the dance routine they'd been practising. When he'd gone, Danni peeped out from behind Kirsty's hair to look at the drums that had been set up in front of the drummer. "They're not mine," she whispered in disappointment.

"And...ACTION!" called the director just then. The backing music began, and Kirsty and Rachel started dancing. They couldn't help noticing the drummer who was nearby. He was flailing around wildly behind the drum kit, not looking at all convincing.

"Cut!" the director shouted, striding over to the drummer. "What on earth are you doing?"

"I can't see out of this robot helmet," a rather muffled voice replied.

"Well, take it off then," the director ordered. "We'll get someone from the make-up team to paint your face alien-green instead."

Rachel nudged Kirsty as the drummer removed his helmet. She'd just spotted a pair of very pointy ears on the drummer's head that looked suspiciously like goblin ears! The girls were finding it more difficult than usual to spot the goblins this time, because Jack Frost had cast a spell on them to make them human-coloured, and much taller. But there was no mistaking those pointy ears and nose!

"He's got big feet too," Kirsty said, bending down to have a quick check. "He's most definitely a goblin!"

Mandy hurried on stage and began dabbing bright green stage make-up all over the goblin's skin. Kirsty and Rachel had to struggle not to giggle at the goblin's expression as his face changed colour. Jack Frost's spell had been for nothing now!

"I don't know about 'alien-green'," Kirsty whispered. "It looks more like goblin-green to me!"

Danni was smiling. "If a goblin is here, it means my Magical Drums are somewhere around too," she whispered excitedly. "Now all we need to do is find them!"

Goodbye, Goblin!

"And... ACTION!" cried the
director a few minutes later. The
music started up again, but this time
there was a *second* drumbeat to be
heard. Kirsty and Rachel stared at
the goblin behind the drum kit.

They knew that the musicians were supposed to be miming for the filming of the video, and should be making no sound. But they could definitely hear the goblin's drumsticks hitting the cymbals and drums!

"He's taken off the muffles," Danni whispered. "No wonder we can hear what he's doing." Kirsty and Rachel could see some muffle pads on the ground, where the goblin had thrown them.

"Cut!" came an impatient shout.

"Here comes the director again," Rachel murmured, "and he doesn't look very happy."

"Put those back on," the director snapped at the goblin. "We're never going to finish this video with you messing about!"

The goblin scowled, but did as he was told.

"And... ACTION!" the director called a third time.

The goblin picked up his drumsticks and began playing again. Now that the muffles were back on, there was virtually no noise to be heard from the drum kit, but the girls could tell that he was playing well and keeping perfect time. Danni began dancing to the rhythm on Kirsty's shoulder, and Rachel could see that she was tapping imaginary drumsticks in excitement.

"He's good," Danni whispered. "My drums *must* be very close by. I'm sure they're helping him play so well."

Kirsty agreed. The Magical Musical Instruments were full of such powerful magic that anyone who was close to them became very skilled at playing that particular instrument. So the Magic Drums had to be very near the goblin indeed – but why couldn't the girls and Danni see them?

A thought struck Kirsty. "What if the Magic Drums are still at their tiny Fairyland size?" she whispered to Danni and Rachel. "The goblin might have them hidden in his pocket!"

All three friends stared at the goblin, who was now making up a spectacular drum solo that didn't fit in with the song or video at all.

"CUT!" yelled the director, who sounded really fed up now. "You're fired," he told the goblin. "Get off the set immediately! We'll use a different actor in your place."

The goblin put his nose in the air.
"I'd rather rehearse with my own band anyway," he retorted, and stormed off the set.

Rachel and Kirsty instinctively made to follow him but the director spotted them.

"Girls – where are you going?" he called. "We need you here, please."

"Sorry," Kirsty said politely. As soon as the director had moved out of earshot, she turned to Rachel in a panic. "What are we going to do? The goblin's getting away!"

"I'll follow the goblin so that we don't lose him," Danni suggested.

"But there are so many people around," Rachel reminded her. "We don't want anyone to see you!"

"We need to create a diversion," Kirsty suggested. "Something that will get everyone looking at us, so that Danni can sneak away without being spotted."

"How about if I pretend to fall over and bump into the drum kit?" Rachel said. "That'll make a lot of noise."

"Good idea," Danni said. "Let's try it."

Rachel sidled closer to the drums and pretended to be practising her dance routine. Then she stumbled deliberately,

so as to knock over the drums with
a huge crash!

Just as the girls had hoped, everyone
turned to look and several people rushed
over to help Rachel.

"Go!" Kirsty whispered, and Danni
whizzed up high into the air.

Out of the corner of her eye, Rachel
just caught sight of a tiny speck zooming
out of the room. Danni had gone.

Where's Danni?

A short while later, the director called for a break, and Rachel and Kirsty were told they could leave the set for half an hour. "At last!" Kirsty said as she and Rachel ran out of the room in search of Danni and the goblin. "I've been dying to know what's been happening."

"I hope Danni's all right," Rachel said as they went along the corridor. "I've hardly been able to concentrate on dancing – I've been thinking about her the whole time."

The girls were near a canteen now and looked in cautiously. There were chairs and tables set up where people were drinking coffee and eating sandwiches, but no sign of a goblin in a robot suit, or a tiny fairy. "Not there," Kirsty said. "Let's check in the dressing and make-up areas."

The girls went down to the room with the clothes rails, then to Mandy's make-up room, but neither Danni nor the goblin were there either. "I hope everything's all right," Rachel said anxiously. "Where can they be?"

"What's that?" Kirsty asked, crouching down to peer at the floor. "Look, Rachel. Glitter!"

Rachel stared at the line of pink glitter along the ground. "I wonder if Danni's left us a glittery trail to follow?" she said, feeling excited.

"There's only one way to find out," Kirsty said, grabbing her friend's hand. "Come on!"

The girls raced down the corridor, following the glittery line. The trail led to a small office on the far side of the warehouse. They peeped around the edge of the door, which was ajar, and saw three goblins gathered around a table. On top of the table was… a tiny drum kit!

"There it is," Rachel hissed, her heart thumping.

The green goblin who'd been in the video was glaring at the drum kit. "Why didn't Jack Frost give us a wand to make this thing bigger and smaller when we need to?" he complained. "How am I meant to practise for the band when my drums are so titchy?"

"Grow!" another goblin ordered the drum kit, pointing at it with a warty finger. "Grow, you stupid thing!"

The drummer goblin took out his drumsticks and started trying to play the drums with them, but he only knocked them over. "Hopeless," he grumbled. "Here, give us a go on your triangle."

Rachel and Kirsty could see that the third goblin had a triangle which he was playing gently. He swung it away protectively at the drummer goblin's words, though. "No," he said. "This is mine!"

Danni appeared by the girls' shoulders just then. "Hi there," she whispered. "I've been hoping for a chance to fly in and grab my drums, but the goblins never move far away enough."

The three friends racked their brains for what to do next.

The goblins were still arguing about playing the triangle…and their bickering suddenly gave Rachel an idea. "Danni, if you could conjure up some musical instruments in a different room, we might be able to lure the goblins out of this one," she said. "Hopefully they'll leave the Magic Drums here in their excitement!"

Danni nodded, smiling. "I could magic up some instruments, but they won't last for long," she said, "only for a few hours. Still – that should be all we need. Let's try it!"

The three of them walked further along the corridor and found an empty room just next door. They went inside and Danni waved her wand. Instantly, a selection of instruments appeared in a line on the floor – a tambourine, a xylophone, a trumpet,

and some guitars and cymbals,
all in bright colours and sparkling
with fairy magic.

"They look great," Kirsty
said, picking up a pink
tambourine and giving it
a shake. "Very funky."

"Let's hope the
goblins are
tempted,"
Rachel said.
"Come on!"
They hurried
back to where the
goblins were still
arguing, and Danni
tucked herself under Rachel's hair.
If the goblins saw that a fairy was
around, they would be very suspicious!

"Good news," cried Kirsty as they entered the room. "We heard you saying you wanted to play some instruments, and I thought you'd like to know there are lots next door."

"A trumpet, a saxophone, a lovely tambourine…" Rachel reeled off. "And you can choose whatever you like!"

"Oooh," said the goblin with the triangle. "That sounds fun."

"Yes," agreed the goblin who didn't have an instrument. "We can make lots of noise!"

Rachel held her breath as she waited
for the drummer goblin to reply.
He didn't look quite so keen. "You two
go," he told his friends. "I'm staying
here to guard my drums."

"Why don't you just take a look?"
Kirsty said persuasively. "They're really
great instruments."

The goblin shook his head stubbornly,
and Rachel and Kirsty could only
exchange helpless glances as they
followed the other two goblins out
of the room. The plan had failed.
What else could they do to get Danni's
drums back?

A Small Surprise

"This way," Rachel told the two excited goblins, who were capering up and down the corridor like little children. She pushed open the door of the next room and both goblins rushed inside.

"Ooh, brilliant!" one squealed, racing over to the green trumpet and blowing into it.

"Look at me!" the second giggled, bashing away at the bright red

xylophone. "Choose whichever one you like," Kirsty said. She caught Rachel's eye. "We'll be back in the other room, OK?"

The two friends hurried out, keen to get back to the goblin with the Magic Drums. On the way, another idea popped into Kirsty's head. "Danni," she said wonderingly, "would you be able to make the goblin really small, so that he was the right size to play your drums?"

Danni fluttered
out from her
hiding place
to hover in front
of Kirsty's face.
"Sure," she said.
"Why?"

"Because then he
won't be able to stop us picking up
your drum kit," Kirsty replied with
a smile.

"Good thinking!" Rachel said.

"Yes, that might work," Danni
agreed. "I like it, Kirsty!"

They went back into the first room,
where the drummer goblin was sitting
in front of the Magic Drums.
"Abracadabra!" he was muttering.
"Hocus Pocus!"

"You're much too big for those drums," Kirsty told him.

"It's not me that's too big, it's these drums that are too small," the goblin grumbled in reply. "If only I could make them bigger... Hey Presto!" he cried, snapping his fingers hopefully. Nothing happened.

"Well," said Kirsty, "my friend here could use *her* magic to make them the right size for you. Then you'd be able to play them properly, wouldn't you?"

The goblin looked at Danni suspiciously. He clearly didn't trust a fairy but seemed desperate to play the Magic Drums. "All right," he

said after a few moments,
obviously expecting Danni
to make the drums bigger.
Danni grinned and waved
her wand…and magicked the
goblin to the size of
a matchstick!

At first, the
goblin didn't
seem to realise
what had
happened. He looked at the drum
kit, saw that it was the right size for
him and gave a yelp of delight. Then
he rushed over and began pounding
away with his drumsticks, which had
shrunk, too.

"Wow, he's good," Rachel said admiringly, as he bashed out a fantastic drum roll.

Danni arched an eyebrow. "Only because my drums are magic," she reminded Rachel. "*They're* doing all the work, not him."

The goblin looked up at the sound of their voices…and did a double take when he saw that the girls now looked like giants! His mouth fell open as the truth hit him. "I've been tricked!" he wailed.

"That's right," Kirsty said cheerfully, reaching down to pick him up.

"Oi!" he squealed. "Put me down!"

"I'll have these, thank you," Rachel said, scooping the Magic Drums into her palm.

The goblin, meanwhile, was kicking his tiny legs and shrieking, "Put me down!" at Kirsty.

"I will," she promised, "just as soon as Danni has her drums back."

Danni soared towards Rachel, her wings shimmering all the colours of the rainbow as she flew. She was just about to land on Rachel's palm when the door flew open, and in came the two other goblins, carrying some of the

colourful instruments from the room next door.

"HELP!" the tiny goblin squeaked to his friends. "They're trying to steal the Magic Drums!"

Off to Goblin Grotto!

Danni tapped her wand on the snare drum in the nick of time. There was a flash of fairy magic, and then a pair of drumsticks appeared in Danni's hand and the Magic Drums flew up into the air with Danni, just as the goblins made a lunge for her. Their long fingers closed around empty air as she darted out of reach.

"Give those back!" the tiny goblin shrieked, his little voice high-pitched and shrill. "I need them for Jack Frost's Gobolicious band!"

Danni shook her head. "These are my drums, and I need them to make music sound good everywhere," she said. "They're not meant for one goblin to use selfishly."

Kirsty set him down on the table and he stamped his foot. "Rotten fairy!" he shouted peevishly.

"Now, now," Danni said, "that's not very nice. I think you should

get back to Goblin Grotto with your
friends before any humans see you.
If you promise to go straight there,
I'll turn you back to your usual size."

The tiny goblin looked very sulky
at her words.

"I'll do no such thing," he said,
putting his little hands on his hips.

Danni looked anxiously at Kirsty and
Rachel. "We can't leave him running
around like this," she said.

Rachel gave her a wink and
reached over to stroke
the tiny goblin's head.
"He's very cute like
this," she said.
"Maybe we
should keep
him as he is?"

Kirsty joined in. "Oh yes," she agreed. "I've got an old doll's house at home. He could live in that!"

"We can dress him up in some doll's clothes too," Rachel said, trying not to giggle. "Won't he look sweet in a dress?"

The tiny goblin was going purple with rage, and his friends were spluttering

with laughter. "All right, all right," he grumbled. "I'll go home. Just turn me back to normal!"

"OK," Danni laughed. She waved her wand again and a swirl of pink sparkles flooded from its tip, streaming all around the miniature goblin. With a faint whooshing sound, he was back to his usual size in a moment. "There," Danni said. "You three can play with the instruments I magicked up for you, but you must take them back to Goblin Grotto."

The goblins nodded. They knew when they were beaten. "All right," they muttered glumly. Then they snatched up the instruments and left.

Danni smiled at Kirsty and Rachel as the door closed behind them. "Thanks, girls!" she cried, swooping down to kiss them each on the cheek. "I'm so happy to have my drums back again…and it's all thanks to your quick wits. Well done!"

"You're welcome," Kirsty said with a smile. "That was fun – did you see the look on the goblin's face when we talked about dressing him up in doll's clothes? I thought he was going to explode!"

"I hope he'll think twice before he agrees to any more of Jack Frost's mean ideas," Danni said. "Now, I'd better get back to Fairyland with my Magic Drums. And you two should get back to the video shoot. I'm sure that now my drums are safely with me, things will run much more smoothly there." She winked. "I think they'll find the instruments will all be working perfectly now."

"Thanks, Danni," said Rachel. "I'm really pleased we could help. Bye!"

The little fairy vanished in a burst of pretty pink sparkles.

The two girls smiled at one another. "That's four of the Magical Musical Instruments we've helped the fairies find," Kirsty said happily, as they began walking back towards the set. "What a magical, musical holiday this is turning out to be!"

Now Rachel and Kirsty must help

Maya the Harp Fairy

Jack Frost's goblins have stolen the Music Fairies' Magical Musical Instruments, so nobody can play music properly! Can Rachel and Kirsty help Maya to find her Magic Harp?

Here's an extract from
Maya the Harp Fairy...

Confetti Surprise

"Isn't this a beautiful place for a wedding?" Kirsty Tate said as she and her best friend, Rachel Walker, bounded up the steps of the Wetherbury Hotel. Kirsty was carrying a large parcel wrapped in sparkly gold paper and tied with a silver bow, and Rachel's arms were full of pink flowers. Both girls were wearing pretty party dresses.

"Oh, yes!" Rachel agreed, glancing up at the old manor house, its stone walls covered in rambling ivy.

"And the gardens are gorgeous too," she added.

The hotel was surrounded by emerald-green lawns and large beds of brightly coloured flowers, and there was a tall stone wall around the edge of the lawns with archways leading to the rest of the grounds.

"Isn't it brilliant that Kerry decided to have her wedding while you're staying with us for half-term, Rachel?" Kirsty remarked as they paused at the top of the steps to wait for Mrs Tate. "That means you can come too!"

Rachel nodded. "It was nice of Kerry to invite us," she replied. "You must have been a really good little girl when she was your babysitter, Kirsty!"

Kirsty laughed. "Here's Mum," she said.

Mrs Tate was hurrying up the steps towards them. "Let's go inside, girls," she said, glancing at her watch. "Kerry's expecting us to be early so we can help with finishing off the decorations for the wedding reception."

The doors into the hotel lobby stood wide open and Rachel gasped with wonder as they went in.

"Wow, this is *lovely!*" she exclaimed. The lobby was painted white and gold and there were huge vases of sweet-smelling roses everywhere. The carpet underfoot was thick, red and velvety, and a glittering glass chandelier hung from the ceiling. In one corner of the lobby was a man in a tuxedo, seated at a baby grand piano, leafing through sheets of music.

"Yes, it's perfect for a wedding, isn't it?" Mrs Tate agreed. "Girls, will you take the present into the reception room? I'll go and find Kerry. Oh, and Rachel, you give me the flowers and take these instead…" She handed a brown bag of confetti packets to Rachel. "Will you two scatter some of this confetti on the tables?"

"OK, Mum," Kirsty agreed, and Mrs Tate hurried off with the flowers. Meanwhile the girls went down a corridor to the reception room.

"What's that noise?" Rachel asked curiously as they got nearer to the open door…

The Music Fairies

Win Rainbow Magic goodies!

In every book in the Rainbow Magic Music Fairies series (books 64-70) there is a hidden picture of a musical note with a secret letter in it. Find all seven letters and re-arrange them to make a special Music Fairies word, then send it to us. Each month we will put the entries into a draw and select one winner to receive a Rainbow Magic Sparkly T-shirt and Goody Bag!

Send your entry on a postcard to Rainbow Magic Music Fairies Competition, Orchard Books, 338 Euston Road, London NW1 3BH.
Australian readers should write to Hachette Children's Books, Level 17/207 Kent Street, Sydney, NSW 2000.
New Zealand readers should write to Rainbow Magic Competition, 4 Whetu Place, Mairangi Bay, Auckland, NZ.
Don't forget to include your name and address.
Only one entry per child.
Final draw: 30th September 2009.

Good luck!

Have you checked out the

website at:
www.rainbowmagic.co.uk

Look out for the
Magical Animal Fairies!

ASHLEY
THE DRAGON FAIRY
978-1-40830-349-8

LARA
THE BLACK CAT FAIRY
978-1-40830-350-4

ERIN
THE FIREBIRD FAIRY
978-1-40830-351-1

RIHANNA
THE SEAHORSE FAIRY
978-1-40830-352-8

SOPHIA
THE SNOW SWAN FAIRY
978-1-40830-353-5

LEONA
THE UNICORN FAIRY
978-1-40830-354-2

CAITLIN
THE ICE BEAR FAIRY
978-1-40830-355-9

Available
April 2009